Witch on a Motorcycle

Witch on a Motorcycle

Written by Marian Frances
Illustrated by Veronica Buffington

Troll Associates

Printed in the United States of America. Troll Associates, Mahwah, N.J.

WITCH ON A MOTORCYCLE

Willie lived at 206 Oak Street, high in the MacGillicuddy's attic. It was a rather nice house made of sturdy wood shingles, on a quiet street in a rather pleasant town.

And all in all Willie was quite content with her life.

She and Tom had fixed up comfortable quarters among the dusty steamer trunks and the old magazines Mr. MacGillicuddy liked to save.

As the warm days of summer turned into the cooler days of autumn, Willie went happily about with her customary ways, of cooking, mending and doing something she especially enjoyed — watching the children.

High in the attic, hidden behind the curtain, she could watch the children at play without being seen. It was one of the reasons she took the attic in the first place.

But as the days grew shorter and chill winds rustled the trees, Willie became increasingly disturbed. In fact, she had a serious problem. What to do? What to do? Willie couldn't quite decide.

Then the day came when Willie had to face her problem squarely. Poor Willie. Halloween was here, and she had lost her broom!

Cousin Charlie thought it was terrible. "No respectable witch ever loses her broom," he said slyly.

Cousin Charlie was a frequent but uninvited guest. And while he talked, Willie looked high and low just to prove her good intentions.

"If you put things back where they belong, you'd know where they were," he said.

It was Willie's misfortune to have a cousin who was always neat, always on time for supper, always doing the right WRONG things.

She was busily looking in dusty pots, opening creaky bureau drawers, just to prove to Charlie that she was serious. But she knew it was impossible because she had looked before.

Poor Willie. She was a flop as a witch. She knew it. Charlie knew it.

In fact, even to this day, Willie had never really gotten used to the idea of sitting on a broom, riding in the sky with all her other relatives.

"This is terrible," said Charlie. "You never do the right WRONG things. Do you want to ruin our reputation in this town?"

Then Charlie got up to go. "Well, I really must fly. Please don't forget, there's a witches' meeting tonight after haunting, and YOU'RE expected to attend. Don't forget."

"Goodbye, Charlie," Willie called after him. "Tom and I will look extra hard for the broom."

Where is a good place to look for a lost broom?

Willie and Tom walked up one street and down the next.

As Halloween night descended on town like a soft blanket of gloomy mist, the wind caused the leaves to make eerie, scratchy sounds.

Willie and Tom made sure to stay together. For one thing, neither of them was especially fond of the flying furry things that kept bumping into them.

Onward, onward they walked, up and down the dark streets, looking on porches and behind trees, but there was no broom anywhere.

Suddenly they stopped in their tracks. Two strange eyes were watching their every move.

Willie looked up. "Excuse me, have you seen my broom?"

"N-o-o-o-o-o. N-o-o-o-o-o," was the reply.

They continued on their lonely way. Tom even ventured down dark alleys to look into trash cans.

This is ridiculous, thought Willie. Here I am on Halloween night . . . stranded.

Then she had an idea. She looked in her pocket, found 35¢, and walked to the hardware store.

She'd prove herself to Charlie after all.

Inside the hardware store she saw lovely things for scaring people. But when she got to the broom section, she stopped short.

"Drats. Cats." She stamped her foot.

Even on the way back home, she looked high and low while Tom sighed gently.

Lights were now beginning to flick on all over town. Things were getting scarier and scarier, and Willie could hear her relatives haunting people in the neighborhood.

EEEEK!
EEEEEK!
EEEEK!
EEEEK!
EEEK!
EEEEEK!

"Oh, I never do anything right. Oh, I never scare anybody."

Then, so Tom wouldn't see, she pulled out her handkerchief and blew her nose heartily, to catch a big tear.

When she got to the MacGillicuddy's house, she was so lonely that she peeked into the window just to see what was going on.

What was going on?

Close to the window, Willie could carefully observe that nothing much was happening.

The grandfather clock in the living room was ticking away the last few hours of Halloween night, and Mr. and Mrs. MacGillicuddy were getting ready for bed.

Then she saw it. Then she saw it. Her broom. Practically falling out of the hall closet. Impossible to reach.

"My broom, my broom," whispered Willie. "Mrs. MacGillicuddy must have taken it down from the attic thinking it was an old MacGillicuddy broom.

MacGillicuddy broom indeed!"

Willie shook her head sadly. What a flop I am. My broom is gone. I have missed the haunting. I will miss the meeting and Charlie will be disturbed. Tomorrow he will say, "Willie, Willie, why can't you do anything right?"

Then she turned to go, and CRASH! She stumbled over something in the dark.

"What's this?" she said, rubbing the bump on her head.

There, in the dark, near the bushes, on this gloomiest of Halloween nights, was a shiny motorcycle.

Willie looked at the big, fast wheels with wide round eyes. Why, on this night of all nights, had Mr. MacGillicuddy forgotten to put away his motorcycle?

In the darkness Willie touched the motorcycle and admired its strong steel handlebars.

She wondered how it would feel to sit on the seat of a motorcycle. She had never been on one before.

Suddenly, she decided she would sit down just for a second. She looked around, held her breath and climbed upon the seat.

It was comfortable!

Then, without warning, the motorcycle started to move.

Willie was frozen with fear. She tried to stop it from rolling down the lawn.

She pulled a switch. The motorcycle roared.

ZOOM. ZOOM. ZOOM.

The motorcycle started going faster and faster.

Willie rocked in the seat, frantically trying to stop the motorcycle.

She pulled another switch. ZOOM. ZOOM. ZOOM. The motorcycle went even faster.

Streets and houses whizzed past her. Everything became a blur. Willie's cape flapped in the wind. ZOOM. ZOOM. ZOOM.

Willie gripped the handlebars for dear life. Suddenly she decided to make the best of a frightening situation. She decided to head for the vacant lot on Center Street where the witches' meeting was in progress. Perhaps they could help her.

ZOOM. ZOOM. ZOOM. Willie rocketed around corners and roared through the streets.

As Willie screeched up Center Street, she could see the witches gathered together, gossiping about their Halloween adventures.

ZOOM. ZOOM. ZOOM. Willie headed right for the vacant lot. She could see Cousin Charlie standing there.

ZOOM. ZOOM. ZOOM. She bounced up the curb and circled round and round the group, unable to stop.

Hanging onto the motorcycle as best she could, she called out to them: "Someone save me. Someone save me. Someone stop this machine."

But round and round she went, her cape flapping in the wind; ZOOM, ZOOM, ZOOM, the motorcycle making its sputtering, roaring sounds.

Needless to say, the witches had never seen such a frightening sight in their lives.

What was this creature who kept screeching round and round them? Whatever it was, it seemed to be coming closer and closer.

What horrible, horrible sounds!

Someone pointed. "Look at those flapping wings." And they all shuddered in fear.

ZOOM. ZOOM. ZOOM.

"It's a prehistoric insect that's come to get us," someone screamed.

"It's come to chew us up in tiny pieces," another wailed. Well, when Cousin Charlie heard that, THUD, he promptly fainted.

ZOOM. ZOOM. ZOOM went Willie, going round and round, hanging on for dear life.

She saw the witches huddled together. Wasn't anybody going to help her stop this motorcycle?

Who was going to help her get off? Couldn't they hear her pleas for help?

She cried out again, "Please, someone help me." But the witches only huddled closer together and held their ears in fright.

The witches watched the creature fly closer and closer. ZOOM. ZOOM. ZOOM. Round and round it went, hissing and snorting and flapping and flying.

"Let's get out of here. Run for your lives," someone called, "before it's too late. Life will be damp and dark and dreary in that creature's belly."

"Let's flee. Let's flee," they called to each other.

And with that, they picked up Cousin Charlie, and flew up and away in all directions.

Well, Willie could hardly believe her eyes when she saw the witches fleeing.

This is ridiculous, she thought. Here I am on Halloween night . . . abandoned.

What do you do when you're abandoned on Halloween night?

Well, since there was no place to go, Willie decided to head home. She turned around. ZOOM. ZOOM. ZOOM. And off she went.

Willie gripped the handlebars as the motorcycle raced noisily up one street and down the next.

ZOOM. ZOOM. ZOOM. As she turned up Oak Street, Willie hit a bump.

"Merciful heavens," she cried. She bounced high in the seat and came down with a thud.

Click. Something happened. Suddenly the motorcycle went slower and slower and slower until it finally stopped.

Willie was delighted to find that her motorcycle trip was over.

She jumped down from the seat and gave a sigh of relief, a great silent sigh of relief.

She rolled the motorcycle back to where she had found it on the MacGillicuddy's lawn, and then dusted it off so no one would know a witch had ridden it.

And there was Tom, waiting for her all this time.

"Oh, Tom, Oh, Tom. What a night I've had. I wonder what Cousin Charlie will say tomorrow.

"My goodness, traveling certainly does broaden your background!

"But for me," she said, as she picked up Tom and held him close. "But for me, there's no place like home... especially with you."